PIRATE SCHOOL
Port of Spies

by Brian James
illustrated by Jennifer Zivoin

Grosset & Dunlap

For all the little pirates in the sea.—BJ

To Katie and Steven, for all of our childhood adventures—whether real or imagined.—JZ

GROSSET & DUNLAP
Published by the Penguin Group
Penguin Group (USA) Inc., 375 Hudson Street, New York, New York 10014, U.S.A.
Penguin Group (Canada), 90 Eglinton Avenue East, Suite 700, Toronto, Ontario, Canada M4P 2Y3
(a division of Pearson Penguin Canada Inc.)
Penguin Books Ltd, 80 Strand, London WC2R 0RL, England
Penguin Ireland, 25 St Stephen's Green, Dublin 2, Ireland
(a division of Penguin Books Ltd)
Penguin Group (Australia), 250 Camberwell Road, Camberwell, Victoria 3124, Australia (a division of Pearson Australia Group Pty Ltd)
Penguin Books India Pvt Ltd, 11 Community Centre, Panchsheel Park, New Delhi - 110 017, India
Penguin Group (NZ), 67 Apollo Drive, Rosedale, North Shore 0745, Auckland, New Zealand
(a division of Pearson New Zealand Ltd)
Penguin Books (South Africa) (Pty) Ltd, 24 Sturdee Avenue, Rosebank, Johannesburg 2196, South Africa

Penguin Books Ltd, Registered Offices:
80 Strand, London WC2R 0RL, England

Library of Congress Control Number: 2007009634

ISBN 978-0-448-44646-2

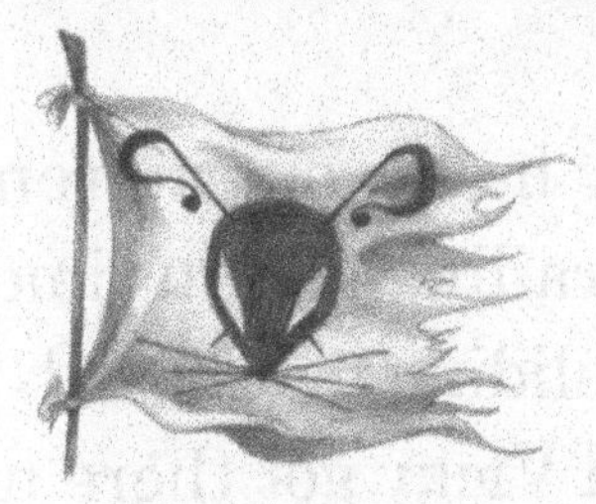

Chapter 1
Anchors Away!

"Arrr! Last one there's a rotten fish!" I shouted to my mates at Pirate School. Then I held on to my pirate hat as I raced across the deck of the *Sea Rat*.

"You better start swimming then, because that's going to be you," Aaron said.

"Not if you slip on the slimy boards," I yelled back.

Racing across the deck was dangerous. It was really easy to slip and crash into a really big *ouch*!

But sometimes, being a pirate meant ignoring danger. Even the *ouch* kind of danger!

This was one of those times.

I stuck my hands out in front of me and grabbed the railing just in time to stop myself from sliding overboard. "I win!"

Aaron and Vicky got there next, at the same time. They're twins, so they do a lot of things the same. They even look the same, only Vicky has long hair.

"I'm second," Aaron said.

"We tied!" Vicky argued.

"Arrr! That's only because I slipped," Aaron grumbled.

I rolled my eyes. Sometimes Aaron was a sore loser.

Just then I saw the most amazing sight. "Shiver me timbers!" I shouted. "There it is! King's Island, dead ahead!"

King's Island was the most famous port in this part of the sea.

"Blimey! It's the biggest town I've ever seen!" Vicky said.

"Aye!" Aaron shouted. Even though Aaron liked to argue with Vicky, he had to agree about King's Island.

"I've been a pirate my whole life, all

nine years and three-quarters, and I've never seen an island like that," I said.

Just then, Gary came running up. He was my best mate at Pirate School. He was also the clumsiest pirate kid on the seas. He slipped right into me!

CRASH!

"Sorry, Pete," he said.

"Arrr! That's okay," I said, helping him up. "If I hadn't stopped you, you would have been shark bait for sure," I said.

"Aye!" Gary said, putting his pirate hat and his glasses back on. He sure was lucky to have a best mate like me!

We went back to looking at King's Island as the *Sea Rat* sailed closer. The island was polka-dotted with stores and houses. They were all painted bright colors. Some were green and others were purple. Some of them were even pink.

"King's Island sure is one pretty place," I said.

"Aye!" my friends agreed.

Then I scratched my head and looked

around. Seeing all the pretty buildings made me think of Inna. Inna *loved* pretty things. But she was nowhere in sight.

"Great sails! Where's Inna?" I shouted. "I know she wouldn't want to miss seeing this!" I was about to go belowdecks to look for her, when all of a sudden she came walking up the galley stairs. She was wearing a fancy dress and her hair was all shiny. She must have taken a bath, because her face looked squeaky clean.

"Arrr! What took you so long?" I asked.

"I was making sure there were no wrinkles in my dress. And then I brushed my hair twice and tied it with a new ribbon," she told us.

"Why'd you do all that?" Aaron asked.

Inna made a huffy noise. "Because I want to look my best when I go into town."

We all rolled our eyes. Inna was the only pirate kid in the whole world who liked to get dressed up.

Inna's big blue eyes got even bigger as she saw the town for the first time. She clapped her hands and shouted, "It's the most beautifulest place ever!"

We couldn't wait until we dropped anchor and got to explore. None of us pirate kids had ever been to King's Island. The ships we had been on before we came to Pirate School never even sailed close to it. But Captain Stinky Beard told the crew that our ship was going to dock there for a whole day to get supplies. Pirates don't get to see big towns very much, so this was going to be a special treat.

"I heard you can get anything you want there," Vicky said.

"Aye!" Gary said. "I heard they have stores that sell fresh-baked cookies!"

Since the ship was low on supplies, we'd been eating seaweed slop for days. Thinking about cookies made my stomach grumble and my mouth a little drooly.

"Arrr! I heard there's a store that sells shiny jewelry," Inna said.

"Oh, barnacles! Who cares about that stuff?" Aaron said. "The best sword-maker in all the seas lives there! I can't wait to get my hands on one of those!" he shouted.

Vicky crossed her arms and rolled her eyes. That's the face she made when Aaron acted like a show-off. And Aaron *always* acted like a show-off. So Vicky made that face a lot.

"I just hope Rotten Tooth doesn't make us stay aboard and scrub dishes," I said.

"AYE!" everyone agreed.

Rotten Tooth was our teacher at Pirate School. He was also the first mate. That meant he was the double boss of us and could give us stinky orders, like making us scrub things.

If it were up to him, we'd never learn any pirate stuff. Good thing Captain Stinky Beard was the boss of him. Pirate School was all the captain's idea, and he made sure ol' Rotten Guts taught us more than just how to be deckhands.

"Arrr! I hope he gives us the day off," Gary said.

"Aye, me too!" Aaron agreed.

"Aye, me three," Inna said.

Vicky hoped so, too. But she didn't want it to look like she was agreeing with Aaron, so she didn't say so. She just nodded her head instead.

Soon our ship sailed closer to the harbor. The harbor was crowded with a whole fleet of ships.

"Avast! There are no other pirate ships," Vicky said.

I took a look around. She was right.

"Arrr! I'm glad!" Inna said. "I don't want any rival pirates messing up my day."

"But sometimes, it's bad luck to be the only pirate ship," Gary told us. "I heard that in a pirate tale once on my old ship."

"Arrr! We don't know for sure if we'll be the only pirates. There might be others on the island in disguise," I said. "Most towns don't really like pirates. So sometimes pirates need to be real sneaky. It's in the pirate code."

"Aye?" my friends asked.

"Aye!" I answered.

I knew all about the pirate code. I had learned the whole thing before I ever even came to Pirate School.

"Aye!" a voice boomed over my shoulder. It was Captain Stinky Beard. "Being sneaky is a smart idea," he said. Then he turned to the crew. "Lower the flag!" he bellowed.

I smiled proudly.

My mates were pretty proud of me, too.

"Good work, me lil' shipmate," Captain Stinky Beard said to me. "It be better to stay out of trouble. We'll get our supplies and then get sailing!"

"Aye aye!" we said.

I leaned forward and took another long look at King's Island. Even if we weren't going to do any piratey stuff like search for treasure, it sure was going to be a fun place to explore once we weighed anchor.

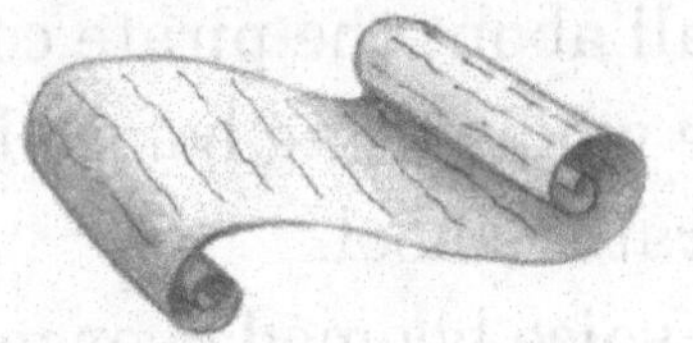

Chapter 2
Part of the Crew

The whole crew headed ashore. Just as we were about to step off the ship, Rotten Tooth stepped in front of us.

Our path was completely blocked.

That's because Rotten Tooth wasn't only the ugliest pirate on the *Sea Rat*, he was also the biggest.

He leaned in so close that his pointy green beard almost poked me. "Arrr! Where do ye mangy sea pups think ye be going?" he growled.

Inna stepped right up to him. She was afraid of lots of stuff, like snakes, and getting dirty. But for some reason, she wasn't at all afraid of Rotten Tooth.

"Arrr! We're going into town with the

rest of the crew," she told him.

"Aye? Is that a fact?" Rotten Tooth said.

"Aye! It's a true fact!" Inna said, folding her arms. "The cap'n says you have to treat us like part of the crew, so there!"

"Aye! Inna's right," Vicky said.

It was true. When the *Sea Rat* was attacked by rival pirates, we saved the day. Even Rotten Tooth said we did a shipshape job. And he promised Captain Stinky Beard that he would treat us like real pirates.

"Aye! I remember," Rotten Tooth admitted. Then he reached into his pocket and took out a really, really, really long list and handed it to us. "That's why I'll be giving ye the ship's shopping list," he said.

I gulped.

It was the longest list I'd ever seen.

I started to read it out loud.

"Four barrels of beef. Ten pounds of butter. Fourteen boxes of candles. Twelve barrels of oatmeal. Twelve barrels of seaweed. Three boxes of soap." I stopped reading when I got to the hog's head because it made me feel sickish. I stuck out my tongue and finally said it out loud.

"Yuck!" Gary said.

Inna's face turned as green as her dress.

"Double yuck!" she yelled.

Vicky grabbed the list from my hand and waved it in Rotten Tooth's face. "Arrr! What's this have to do with being a pirate?" she asked.

"Aye!" Aaron shouted. "Pirates are supposed to swashbuckle, not shop!" Then he started jumping all around and swinging his arms again like he was holding a sword. Only he wasn't watching where he was swinging, and he swung his arm right into Rotten Tooth.

Rotten Tooth picked Aaron up with one hand and growled.

"Uh-oh! I think we're in big trouble," Gary whispered to me.

"Aye, matey! Really giant trouble," I whispered back.

Rotten Tooth looked even madder than the time Aaron made him fall into the fish-gut tank. I thought for sure he was going to toss Aaron right into the sea.

But then Rotten Tooth didn't look so mad anymore. He put Aaron down. He took the list back from Vicky and put it in his pocket. "Arrr! A promise be a promise. And I promised to treat ye pollywogs like one of the crew," he said.

I couldn't believe my eyes and ears!

We were going to be able to explore King's Island after all!

We all smiled. Then we started to walk down the gangway. We got halfway down before Rotten Tooth stopped us again.

"But before ye go, I have a little Pirate School lesson for ye," Rotten Tooth said. He reached into his pocket and took out the list again. "In a pirate crew, the newest recruits always do the shopping! Now get to it!" he shouted, shoving the list into my hand.

We all moaned and groaned. Sometimes being part of a pirate crew was tough work!

"Arrr! And another thing," Rotten Tooth said as we headed ashore. "Keep ye eyes and ears open. Landlubbers be very suspicious of pirates . . . especially wee pirate kids."

Chapter 3
Shop Till You Drop!

"Yo-ho-ho!" I shouted when we walked into the general store. I was really excited. "This is the biggest store I've ever been in!"

"Aye," Vicky agreed. "We wouldn't even be able to fit all of this stuff on the *Sea Rat*!"

There were rows and rows of shelves stretching from wall to wall. They were piled high with all kinds of food. Some I'd never heard of before, like a giant orange thing called a pumpkin.

"Avast! They even have toys!" I said, pointing to a shelf on the far wall. It was filled with toy ships.

"Gangway!" Aaron shouted, and rushed toward the toy section.

He didn't get very far, though, because

Vicky grabbed hold of his belt. "Aren't you forgetting something?" she asked, taking out the shopping list.

"Soggy sails, Vicky's right," I said. "We have to do the shopping or we'll never finish before it's time to set sail."

"Then let's hurry," Inna said. "If we finish early, we might have time to come back."

"Aye, good thinking!" Aaron said.

We started in the first row of shelves and picked out anything that was on the list. Then we went to the next row and did the same thing. By the time we got to the third row, I started to get the feeling that someone was following us. I was just about to check when Gary got my attention.

"Pete! Do we need any of these things?" he asked.

I turned my head and saw Gary standing next to a stack of oranges. He picked up the top one to show me.

I checked the list.

"Nope, no oranges on the list," I said.

"You can put that back."

Gary leaned over to put the orange back on top of the pile. But he leaned too far and the oranges started to wobble. I rushed over, but before I could stop them . . . *WHOOSH!*

All the oranges tumbled over and rolled across the floor.

"You dirty urchins! Look what you've done!" an old man yelled. He was the shopkeeper, and he didn't look very happy.

"I'm sorry," Gary said.

"Aye, we'll clean it up," I promised.

The old man grumbled as Gary and I started to pile up the oranges. "I should throw you out of my store," he said.

"But we're going to buy all of this stuff," Inna told him.

The old man looked at the supplies we'd gathered. "That stuff costs money," he said.

Inna reached into her pocket and took out a bunch of gold coins. The old man didn't seem as mad after that. But he still watched us closely until we were done stacking the oranges. Then we grabbed our stuff, paid, and left.

"Rotten Tooth was right. Some people don't like us pirate kids," I said to Gary.

"Aye!" Gary said back.

"Arrr! Maybe he just doesn't like pirate kids who knock things over," Aaron said.

"It's not my fault," Gary said. "Those oranges were slippery."

"Arrr! Hogwash," Aaron told him. "You knocked that stuff over because you're a blunder head."

Vicky dropped the stuff she was carrying. Then she put her hands on her hips and made a growl. She didn't like it one bit when Aaron acted like he was better than everyone else.

"Arrr! Sometimes you're a blunder head, too!" Vicky said.

"I've never blundered in my life," Aaron said. Then he lifted his chin and half-closed his eyes to make his know-it-all face. He made that face a lot.

Vicky made a huff. "Arrr! What about the time on our old ship when we were playing and you blundered overboard? Or the time here at Pirate School when you blundered into the fish-gut tank?"

Aaron's face turned a little reddish. "I guess that was pretty daft," he admitted.

"Aye, that's what I thought, Captain Big Mouth!" Vicky said.

"Quit bellyaching!" Inna shouted at them. Then she went all quiet. "Everyone is staring at us," she whispered.

I took a look around.

Some of the townspeople were standing around watching us. Other people were watching us from inside the stores. And still more people were watching us from their windows.

"Arrr, everyone act normal," I whispered.

"Aye aye," my friends whispered back.

So we started acting normal. We did things that normal, non-pirate people did. I started to whistle and tap my head. Vicky walked in circles. Aaron and Gary put their hands in their pockets and kicked at stones on the dirt road. Inna walked over to the dress shop and smooshed her face against the window to look at all the dresses.

After a while, the landlubbers stopped staring at us.

I wiped my forehead and sighed. "That was a close one," I said.

"Aye," Vicky said. "We almost forgot the sneaky part of our mission."

"What mission?" Aaron asked. "Rotten Face only sent us to get this stuff because he didn't want to do it himself!"

"Aye," I said. "But Rotten Tooth also

told us to keep our eyes and ears open. That means we have to start spying. It's our secret duty."

"Aye aye!" Gary said. Then he scratched his head. He always did that when he was thinking really hard. "Pete?" he asked. "What are we spying for again?"

I called everyone over and we made a huddle.

Then I made sure no one was spying on us.

The coast was clear, so I whispered real quiet, "We're spying for rival pirates."

Everyone gulped! Rival pirates were serious business.

Aaron made a fist. "If I see any of those pirates, I'll show them who's boss of the seas!" he said in a loud whisper.

Vicky rolled her eyes. "Blimey! You won't see them, because they'll be in disguise, blunder head!"

"Oh, yeah," Aaron said. "I forgot."

"Vicky's right," I said. "They'll be sneaky like us. We have to look for anything suspicious and report it back to the ship."

"I vote we look in the jewelry store," Inna said.

"I vote we look in the sword store," Aaron said.

"I vote we look in every store," I said.

"Aye aye!" everyone agreed.

We put our hands in a circle and whispered our pirate cheer. "Swashbuckling, sailing, finding treasure, too. Becoming pirates is what we want to do!"

We picked up the boxes and headed into the candle store. The lady in that store gave us a mean look as soon as we walked in. In fact, everyone in the store gave us mean looks. I was starting to think that King's Island was full of spies!

Chapter 4
I Spy!

"That seems pretty suspicious to me," I said when we walked by a hat store. "They don't have a single pirate hat, only tall hats and straw hats."

"That is pretty strange," Vicky said.

"Aye, it means other pirates must have bought them all," Inna said. Then she started to make a list of suspicious things.

Next we passed a store that sold maps.

Aaron stopped to look. He squinted his eyes and looked real close. "Sink me! There's not even one treasure map in there."

"Who would want a map if it didn't show you where treasure was?" Gary asked.

Vicky shrugged her shoulders.

"Aye, it doesn't make sense," I said.

"Maybe those pirates who bought all the pirate hats got the treasure maps, too!" Inna said.

"Aye, that makes sense," I said.

Inna sure was one smart pirate. She added the part about the maps to the list, too.

Just then, I thought I saw a pair of eyes peeking at us from a doorway. "Arrr! I think we're being followed," I whispered.

"By who?" Gary asked. Then he turned around to check.

Vicky nudged him. "Don't look, blunder head," she whispered. "You'll give us away."

"Aye," I said. "I think we've been followed into every store."

"Blimey! Why didn't you tell us?" Inna asked.

"Because I wasn't sure," I explained.

I made a *shh* noise to my friends and sneaked over to where I saw the peeking. I took a deep breath and jumped around the corner.

No one was there.

"Maybe it was nothing," Vicky said.

"Or maybe it was a spy and they spied you coming and sneaked off," Inna said.

"I don't know what it was. But there's definitely something fishy about this town, and it isn't just the smelly fish market."

"Aye," my mates agreed, and we kept walking.

By the time we walked past the bakery, we were starving. It was hard work looking for suspicious stuff and shopping at the same time. So we decided to buy some cookies to keep up our strength.

Just to be safe, we asked Gary to wait outside with the boxes.

"Mmm," Inna said as we walked in. "It smells delicious!"

"Aye!" I said. Then I reached for a cookie sitting on the counter.

"Don't touch!" a lady yelled from behind the counter.

We all jumped back.

I could tell by her face that she didn't

like us at all. The corners of her mouth were droopy and her eyes were buggy.

"But . . . we just wanted to buy some cookies," I said.

The lady picked up a rolling pin and waved it in the air. "I know what you wanted! You wanted to steal my cookies!" she shouted.

"No we didn't!" Aaron shouted. "We were going to pay for them!"

"Liar! Thief! You stole a cookie, didn't you?" the lady shouted.

We gulped!

"Let's get out of here," Vicky said.

"Aye!" I agreed. "That lady's crazy!"

We ran outside and picked up the boxes.

"What's going on?" Gary asked.

"We'll tell you later, mate," Vicky said. "But now . . . just *run*!"

We ran as fast as we could, but the lady from the bakery was running after us. "Thieves! Thieves!" she yelled.

Soon there were a whole bunch of townspeople chasing us. My heart was beating at top speed. If they caught us, they'd find out we were pirates. And if they found out we were pirates, we'd be in big trouble.

"Follow me!" Aaron shouted. He turned the corner and we all went after him.

Then . . . *CRASH!*

I bumped right into Aaron. Vicky bumped into me. Then Inna and Gary bumped into Vicky.

"Dead end," Aaron said, staring at the wall in our path.

"Follow *you*? I should have known better," Vicky said to Aaron.

But there was no time to argue, because just then the crowd came around the corner. We were trapped.

"You're in big trouble now," one man said.

"Yeah, we don't like thieves on King's Island," another one said.

Inna stepped up to them. "We're not thieves!" she shouted.

"Aye!" Aaron shouted. "We're pirates!"

Vicky clasped her hand over Aaron's mouth. "That's supposed to be a secret!"

"Oh, yeah," Aaron mumbled into Vicky's hand. "Sorry, mateys! We're just sailors."

"Arrr! It's too late now, Captain Big Mouth," Vicky said.

"Pirates!" the lady from the bakery shouted. "Pirates aren't welcome on King's Island! All pirates are thieves!"

"That's not true," Inna said. "We paid for all this stuff."

"Aye," I said. "Just ask the shopkeepers, they'll tell you."

I saw someone push through the crowd. Maybe it was a rival pirate coming to snatch us away. But when he made his way to the front, I could see that he was a boy like me.

He had blond hair like me. And he was just as tall as me. But he wasn't wearing pirate clothes like me.

"Leave them alone," the boy said. "These are my friends."

"But they're pirates," one of the men said.

The boy laughed. "They're not *real* pirates. We're only playing pirates."

The grown-ups made huffy noises. "We should have known," one grumbled. "Silly kids," another one said. Then one by one they started to leave. Even the lady from the bakery left after we showed her that we didn't steal any cookies.

"Why did you stick up for us?" I asked.

"Because," he said, "I've never seen any real live pirate kids before. In fact, I want to be a pirate when I grow up. I want to be the captain of my own ship one day," he told us. "Captain Jack, because that's my name."

"Aye, me too!" I said. Then I jumped up and down. "Only my name's Pete, not Jack!" I told him.

We were all happy to meet Jack. He was the first person on King's Island who didn't give us dirty looks. Plus, he wanted to know all about being a pirate and going to Pirate School.

"Have you ever found any treasure?" Jack asked.

"Aye! Shiny treasure," Inna said. She showed Jack her necklace and told him that it was from the first treasure she ever found.

"Have you ever seen any sea monsters?" Jack asked.

I shook my head.

"But we did fight a giant snake once!" Gary said.

Inna gave Gary a mean look. Inna absolutely, positively hated snakes more than anything in the world. "Arrr! I told you not to bring up that snake ever again!"

"Sorry. I forgot," Gary said.

Jack wanted to know all about it, but it was getting late.

"Arrr! We have to get back to the *Sea Rat*," I said.

"Aye, we have to report all the strange things we saw," Inna said.

"Our whole ship might be in danger," Gary added.

"Then you'd better hurry," Jack said. "I'll show you a shortcut."

"Thanks, matey!" I said.

"Aye, you're not so bad for a landlubber," Aaron added.

"And you're not so bad for a big mouth," Jack added.

That made us all giggle. Except for Aaron, who frowned.

Then Jack showed us the way back to the docks. He waved good-bye as we boarded the ship. We waved, too, and promised to visit if we ever came back to King's Island again.

Chapter 5
Rotten Report

Rotten Tooth was waiting for us on the deck of the *Sea Rat*. We formed a straight line in front of him. Then we gave him a salute. Even if he was mean and rotten, he was still our teacher.

"Pirate Pete reporting for duty," I said.

Rotten Tooth scratched his pointy beard and flashed a green-toothed smile. "Arrr! Did ye sprogs get everything on the list?"

"Aye aye!" Vicky said.

"Every last thing," Inna said. Then she pinched her nose. "Even the hog's head," she told him.

Rotten Tooth went over to the boxes and started to count them. But pirates aren't very good at counting, so he stopped at five. "Arrr! I'll take ye word for it," he said.

Then he told us we were dismissed for the day.

"Arrr! But don't you want to hear our report?" I asked.

Rotten Tooth looked confused. "What report be that?" he asked.

I looked at Vicky and made a silly face. She covered her mouth to hide a giggle.

"He forgot about the sneaky part of our mission," I whispered.

Only I didn't whisper it quietly enough, because Rotten Tooth heard me. He had the best hearing on the ship. Sometimes I thought he could hear things that hadn't even been whispered yet.

"Arrr! What's this about a sneaky part?" he asked.

"You told us to keep our eyes and ears open," I reminded him. "We did! And we saw a lot of suspicious stuff," I said.

"Aye! We think there are rival pirates on King's Island," Gary added. "We think they might have followed us around."

Rotten Tooth started to snicker. He didn't believe us. So Inna pulled the list from her pocket. She stepped up to Rotten Tooth and showed it to him. "Aye, and here's the proof!" she said.

Rotten Tooth started to read the list.

Then he started to laugh. Soon he was laughing so hard, he filled the sails.

"What's so funny?" Aaron asked.

Rotten Tooth folded the list and tried his best to stop laughing. "Ye scurvy litter have a wild imagination," he said. He said there was nothing suspicious about the stuff on our list.

"Aye? What about the hat store?" I asked.

"Aye! And the map store?" Aaron added.

"Aye, and the mean looks?" Gary asked.

Rotten Tooth laughed again. Then he told us that those stores sell things for landlubbers, not pirates. "And all landlubbers think pirates be a bit dirty. That's why they gave you dirty looks. Ye savvy?"

I thought about that. I reached under my

pirate hat and scratched my head. I guess landlubbers wouldn't need pirate hats or treasure maps.

"Soggy sails," I moaned. "All our spying was for nothing!"

"Stow that talk, little matey!" a voice boomed.

I looked up and saw Captain Stinky Beard standing next to Rotten Tooth. I gave him a quick salute and he saluted back.

"Let me see that," he said to Rotten Tooth. Rotten Tooth handed the captain our list. Captain Stinky Beard read it very carefully.

We all gave each other nervous looks. We were afraid he would start laughing, too.

"Hmm! King's Island has been known to have its share of spies," he said after a while. Then he scratched his beard and gave us a serious look. "This is a shipshape list," he said. "Good work, buckoes."

We were all so happy that we almost started dancing. But it's not real piratey to dance in front of the captain, so we didn't. We just clapped our hands and smiled.

Captain Stinky Beard folded the list and gave it back to Rotten Tooth. "Arrr! Ye better keep an eye out in case any of these spies try to stow away on board," he said. "And ye kids can help, too."

"Aye aye!" we said excitedly. It was our first mission that came directly from the captain.

"Aye, Cap'n!" Rotten Tooth said, only he didn't sound as happy as us.

When the captain left, Rotten Tooth made an angry face and crumpled up our list before shoving it in his pocket. Then he mumbled and grumbled. He thought our list was a waste of time. That was fine with us, so long as the cap'n didn't think so.

As the *Sea Rat* got ready to set sail, we were prepared to take on our new duty. We were going to search the ship for spies!

Chapter 6
Stowaway On Board?

The next day at sea, Rotten Tooth made us stock the storage room with the fresh supplies. He said it was the job of the newest members of a pirate crew. I started to think he was going to use that excuse for every boring job on the ship.

"This stinks!" Vicky said.

Gary made a sniffy face. "I don't smell anything," he said.

"Arrr! I mean this job is no fun!" Vicky said.

"Aye! You can say that again!" Inna said. She was in a grumpy mood because Gary had spilled a bag of flour. It was all in her hair and on her dress.

"Aye! How are we supposed to search

for spies when we're stuck stocking shelves?" Aaron said. Then he folded his arms and plopped down on one of the boxes.

"Maybe if you helped, we'd get done faster!" Vicky said.

"I am helping!" Aaron said.

"Are not!" Vicky shouted.

"Am too!" Aaron yelled back. "I'm supervising!"

Vicky marched right over to Aaron. "Who made you the boss, Captain Big Mouth?"

"I did," Aaron said.

I didn't like it when my mates fought. I jumped between them just as Vicky was giving Aaron a shove.

I crashed right into the pile of supplies!

Vicky rushed over to help me. "I'm sorry, Pete," she said.

"That's okay," I said. "It didn't hurt."

As I stood up, I saw that one of the

barrels of oatmeal was already open.

"Avast! That's a clue!" I shouted.

"A clue that Vicky's just as clumsy as Gary?" Aaron said.

"Blimey! Not that!" I said, and pointed to the open barrel. *"That!"*

"Arrr! It might have been made by a pirate spy!" Vicky said.

"Or maybe it's just a mouse," Gary said.

Inna gave him a mean look. "I told you not to bring up mice!"

Gary scratched his head. "You said not to bring up snakes."

"Same thing! They're both icky!" Inna shouted.

"Shh! I think I heard something," I told them. There was a creaking sound by the door to the storage room.

"Arrr! Maybe one of the spies from town followed us on board," Vicky said.

We all crept toward the door.

I took a peek into the hallway and thought I saw someone. I held up my hand for everyone to stop. "On the count of three, we'll jump out," I whispered.

"Aye aye!" they said.

Then we all counted quietly.

"One. Four. Three!"

We all jumped out into the hallway. And we came face-to-face with . . . Clegg!

"Ahoy there!" Clegg said.

Clegg was the oldest pirate on the *Sea Rat*. He was also our friend. He always told us great pirate stories. But right now, we didn't want to hear a story. We just wanted to know if he saw anyone snooping around.

"Ahoy," I said. "Did you see anyone else out here?"

"Arrr! Just ye little shipmates. But I don't see much," he said, tapping his eye patch. Clegg only had one good eye.

I made a frowny face.

"Who are ye looking for?" he asked.

"A stowaway," I told him.

"Aye?" Clegg asked.

"Aye! A sneaky, spying stowaway!" Vicky said.

"Or a mouse?" Gary said. Then he covered his mouth real quick as Inna glared at him.

"Well, I'll be sure to keep one eye out for the critter," Clegg promised.

"Thanks," I said.

Then we went back to stocking the shelves. We stocked them as fast as we could. As soon as we were done, we were going to look for the stowaway. If there was one on board, we'd find him!

Chapter 7
Pillow Proof!

Searching for spies was hard work. After the shelves were stocked, Rotten Tooth gave us the afternoon off. He said we could do whatever we wanted as long as we stayed out of his way. So we searched the ship for spies.

We searched above deck and belowdecks.

We searched the cargo hold and all the cabins. We even searched Captain Stinky Beard's cabin by peeking through the windows at the back of the ship.

We searched the crow's nest and the quarterdeck. We even searched the poop deck. That was the hardest searching, because we couldn't stop giggling. That deck is one funny deck.

We searched all day long, and by bedtime, we were really tired.

"Arrr! I'm tuckered out," I said as we headed to our quarters.

"Aye, me too!" Aaron said. "I just hope Inna doesn't keep us awake with her snoring!"

"I do *not* snore!" Inna said.

We all rolled our eyes. Inna might be one of the smallest members of the crew, but she was the loudest snorer on the ship! But we were all too sleepy to argue with her.

Vicky jumped onto her bunk and put her head down. Aaron climbed onto the bunk above hers and did the same. Inna had her own bed and she climbed into it.

I had the other top bunk, and Gary's was under mine. He used to have the top one, but he kept rolling off, so we switched.

"Good night, mates," I said as I climbed up.

"Good night," they mumbled.

I put my head down on my pillow and closed my eyes. I was just about to set sail for dreamland when Gary's head popped over the side of my bed.

"Pete?" he said, tapping me awake. I opened one eye to look at him. "I think that stowaway mouse has been sleeping in my bed."

"Aye? Why do you think that?" I asked.

"Because my pillow and my blanket are missing," he said.

I rolled over and peeked down at Gary's bunk. "Shiver me timbers!" I said. Not only were Gary's pillow and blanket missing, there were also oatmeal crumbs on his bunk!

"Arrr! What's all the shouting about?" Vicky asked.

"Aye! I'm

trying to get my beauty sleep," Inna said.

"It's the stowaway! He's been sleeping in Gary's bunk!" I shouted.

Aaron leaped from his bed ready to fight. "Arrr! Where is the slimy stinker?" he shouted.

I shrugged. "Gone," I told him.

"What should we do?" Vicky asked.

"Should we tell Rotten Tooth?" Gary asked.

"Blimey! He won't believe us!" Aaron said.

"Aye, Aaron's right," I said.

"Aye?" Aaron asked. He wasn't used to anyone but himself saying he was right. But this time he was positively correct.

"Aye," I said. "We need to catch this spy by ourselves. We need proof."

"But how are we going to catch the spy?" Gary asked.

"With a really good plan," Inna said.

"Aye!" we agreed.

"But what is the plan?" Gary asked.

"The first part of the plan is to go to

sleep," Inna said. "Then we can think of the second part of the plan in the morning."

I yawned. That sounded like a good plan to me.

Before going back to bed, we put our hands in a circle and said our cheer. "SWASHBUCKLING, SAILING, FINDING TREASURE, TOO. BECOMING PIRATES IS WHAT WE WANT TO DO!"

We all climbed back into bed.

I put my head down again and closed my eyes.

"Psst! Pete?" Gary whispered, poking his head up again. "Can I share your pillow?" he asked. "And your blanket?"

"Sure thing, matey." I yawned. "Sharing is what best mates do best." I rolled over and Gary climbed up to my bunk. Then I was finally able to get some shut-eye.

Chapter 8
Pirate-Proof Plan

As soon as the sun woke up, so did I. But it wasn't the sun that made me open my eyes. I woke up because of the loud noises under my bunk.

THUMP! CRASH!

I sat right up.

"It's the stowaway!" I shouted.

Aaron and Vicky sat up, too. Inna pulled back the pink curtain that hung around her bed. We all looked around, but we didn't see an intruder.

"Arrr! It's only me," Gary said as he stood up and put his glasses back on. He'd fallen off the bunk again.

"Great sails! We should've known," Aaron said.

"Aye," Inna said. "But now that we're all awake, we should think of a way to catch the real stowaway."

"Aye!" the rest of us agreed.

Then we all started thinking as hard as we could. But our stomachs all started to grumble. So none of us could think about anything except breakfast.

"Avast! That's it!" I said. "The stowaway must be hungry, too. If we leave food in here and set a trap, we can catch him!"

"Good thinking, Pete," Vicky said.

"Aye! We can set up a trap with rope and use a blanket as a net. That way, when the stowaway grabs the food, the trap will go off and swoop him up in the blanket," Inna said.

We all agreed that Inna's plan was unsinkable.

We hurried to the mess hall. I could sniff out that we were having oatmeal. "That's perfect," I said. "We know that the spy likes oatmeal."

We all gobbled down our grub. Each of us saved a few spoonfuls, and we spooned that into one bowl. Then we sneaked the bowl back to our quarters. It was a ship rule that no food was allowed out of the mess hall, but this was important.

Lucky for us, Vicky knew all about setting traps.

She tied one end of the rope to the bowl using a special slip knot we'd learned in Pirate School. Then we swung the other end over the roof beams. We knotted four more ropes to that one rope, one for each corner of the blanket.

"When the bowl is picked up, it will set off the trap," Vicky said. "The blanket will swoop up in the air like a net . . . then *WHAM! Gotcha!*"

The sun was getting brighter outside the porthole.

"We'd better hurry on deck for school before Rotten Tooth comes looking for us!" I said.

We ran up the galley stairs to report for duty. We hoped we'd have that spy trapped by the time we came back!

Chapter 9
Trapped!

"Arrr! Ye barnacles better start paying attention!" Rotten Tooth growled. He was trying to teach us how to spot reefs. Only we were all too busy thinking about our trap to concentrate.

"Aye aye!" we said.

"That's more like it," Rotten Tooth said. Then he pointed out to sea. He said that the color of the water warned pirates of reefs.

"Do you think the spy is trapped yet?" Vicky whispered.

Rotten Tooth stopped talking and glared at us. "Spotting reefs might just keep ye pups from sinking to the bottom of the sea one day," he sneered.

"Aye aye!" we said.

When Rotten Tooth wasn't looking again, I leaned over to Vicky. "Spotting spies might keep us afloat, too," I said.

"ARRR! That's it! Ye have sunk your own ship!" Rotten Tooth barked. "School's over! Go to your quarters and don't come out till grub time."

Most of the time, being punished made us frowny. But this time it made us smile, because our quarters were exactly where we wanted to go!

We did our best to hide how happy we were. We pretended to mope until we got to the galley stairs. Once we were out of Rotten Tooth's sight, we let out a loud "Hooray!" and skipped to our room.

Then I made a *shh* noise and sneaked over to our door.

Vicky sneaked behind me and Aaron sneaked behind her.

Inna sneaked, too. But she covered her eyes with her fingers in case there was something creepy in the net.

Gary didn't sneak at all. That's because Gary is a loud sneaker, and this was a job for quiet sneaking.

"Blimey!" I said. "The trap worked!"

"Aye!" Vicky shouted.

The blanket was hanging from the roof beams and something was wiggling inside.

Aaron grabbed a broom from the closet. "Arrr! I'll swashbuckle the spy with this!"

"Arrr! Maybe we should peek to see what it is first," I said.

"Aye, it might just be somebody clumsy like me," Gary said.

"Well, let's find out, buckoes!" I said.

Aaron gripped the broom tighter.

Vicky and Gary held their breath.

Inna covered her eyes tighter.

I started to untie the knot.

Then . . . *THUMP!*

The blanket fell to the ground and opened.

"ARRR!" I screamed.

"AHHH!" the spy screamed back.

We all blinked and rubbed our eyes.

We couldn't believe what we were seeing! Our friend Jack from King's Island was standing in our quarters!

"What in the name of the seven seas are you doing here?" I asked.

Just then a heavy hand came down on my shoulder and I made a double gulp!

"Arrr! That's what I would like to know!" Rotten Tooth growled. Jack trembled with fear. Rotten Tooth could be one scary pirate if he wanted to.

"But . . . but . . . how did you know?" I stuttered.

"The cap'n ordered me to keep my eyes open for anything suspicious. And ye kiddos were acting mighty suspicious this morning," he said. As mean as he was, that Rotten Tooth sure was one clever pirate!

"What's going to happen to me?" Jack asked.

"Arrr! Same thing that happens to all stowaways," Rotten Tooth said. "You are going to walk the plank!"

Chapter 10
Sink or Sail?

Rotten Tooth picked up Jack with one hand and carried him out of our quarters.

"Stop!" Inna shouted. "He's our friend!"

"Gangway! He's a spy!" Rotten Tooth said as he marched up to the main deck.

Jack had saved us from the townspeople, so we had to find a way to save Jack.

There was only one person aboard the *Sea Rat* who could make Rotten Tooth change his mind. So I raced off to the captain's quarters to find Captain Stinky Beard. Aaron, Vicky, Gary, and Inna grabbed hold of Rotten Tooth's legs to try and slow him down.

"Cap'n! Cap'n!" I shouted as I rushed into his office.

Captain Stinky Beard was sitting at his big desk, plotting our course on a huge map. He looked up when I burst in. "Arrr, what is it, my little shipmate?" he asked.

"You have to come quick!" I said. "Rotten Tooth is going to turn one of our friends into shark bait!"

I grabbed the captain's hand and led him onto the main deck. Jack was standing on the plank, and Rotten Tooth was ordering him to march. The whole crew was gathered around to watch.

"Hold it!" Captain Stinky Beard yelled out, and everyone turned to look. He walked over to the plank and demanded to know what was going on.

"Arrr! These pollywogs caught a spy stealing supplies and now they want to save him!" Rotten Tooth said. "I told ye they were too softhearted to be pirates!"

Captain Stinky Beard scratched his beard. "Hmm," he muttered. "The pirate code does say all spies must walk the plank."

"But I'm not a spy!" Jack pleaded.

"Aye! He's not a spy at all!" Inna said.

"Aye!" Aaron said. "He's a landlubber we met on King's Island."

"A landlubber?" Captain Stinky Beard said with a gasp.

"Yep!" Jack said. "I didn't mean to cause any trouble. I just wanted to see what it was like to be a real pirate kid."

"Aye! It's a true fact," I said.

Rotten Tooth groaned. "Arrr! Don't trust him, Cap'n. He's a spy, plain as day!"

Captain Stinky Beard flashed Rotten Tooth a mean look. "Stow it," he said. "If ye had listened to our little shipmates in the first place, ye would have found the boy before we left port. Now we have to figure out what to do with him."

"Please don't make him walk the plank, sir!" we begged.

"No, no!" said Captain Stinky Beard. "I'll not have any kids walking the plank on me ship. He either stays or goes home."

Rotten Tooth leaned in close to Jack. "Arrr! I'm guessing you're going to tell us how you'll be wanting to stay here and go to Pirate School," he said.

But Jack shook his head. "No, thanks!" he said. "I just want to go home. Pirate life is too dirty. Plus, the food is *terrible*!"

"All right, then, home it is," Captain Stinky Beard said. "All hands, man the sails. Full reverse back to King's Island!"

Jack was saved!

"HIP! HIP! HOORAY!" we shouted. Jack shouted it the loudest. Then he came over and thanked us for saving him.

"Arrr! That's what best mates do," I said.

Then Jack thanked the cap'n.

Captain Stinky Beard patted him on the head. Then one by one, the crew returned to their duties. And when Captain Stinky Beard returned to his quarters, Rotten Tooth returned to being mean.

"Ye sprogs better stay

out of my sight!" he yelled. He was steamed that we had gone straight to the captain. "Ye will be getting extra rotten lessons for this!"

When Rotten Tooth left, Jack apologized for getting us into trouble. "I hope you're not mad at me," he said.

"Are you kidding?" Aaron said. "A swell adventure is always worth getting into a little trouble."

"AYE!" the rest of us agreed.

Slowly the ship started to turn around and sail back to King's Island. Jack promised us that when we got to port, he'd show us around. "If it's okay with your captain," he said.

"I think it might be, as long as we ask him really nice," I said. "Our cap'n is always fair."

"Aye," my friends agreed.

I kept my eye on the horizon. I couldn't wait to get there and explore that place again. And this time, the only thing we'd have to shop for would be Inna's shiny bracelet.